NOTHING

NOTHING CAN SEPARATE YOU FROM GOD'S LOVE!

Written by Natalee Creech

and Illustrated by Joseph Cowman

WORTHY® kids

ISBN: 978-0-8249-5703-2

WorthyKids
Hachette Book Group
1290 Avenue of the Americas
New York, NY 10104

Library of Congress CIP data on file

Designed by Eve DeGrie

Printed and bound in China
RRD-SZ_Jan19_1

To my parents, John and Valerie, my first example of God's love.
And to my children, Benjamin and Isadora, remember the promise: nothing can separate you from God's love. ~N.C.

To my three amazing children: Savannah, Alina, and Phoenix.
Love the adventure and let nothing stand in your way! ~J.C.

NOTHING can separate us from
God's love in Christ Jesus our Lord:
not death or life, not angels or rulers,
not present things or future things,
not powers or height or depth,
or any other thing that is created.
—ROMANS 8:38–39 CEB

Can ANYTHING separate me from GOD'S LOVE?

Not mountain
or valley,

not the deepest of seas,

not a rainstorm
or hailstorm

or a cold winter freeze.

Not a rumbling **volcano**,
not an **earthquake** or **flood**,

not a swirling **tornado**
or a **sinkhole** of mud.

There is **nothing** so POWERFUL,
nothing so STRONG—
GOD'S LOVE is too HIGH
and too DEEP
and too LONG!

If I hopped on a **train**

and I rode it **all night,**

if I boarded a plane

for an **overseas flight**,

if I soared in a **rocket**
past planets **in space**,

could I ever **outdistance**
GOD'S LOVE and GOD'S GRACE?

No!

There is **nothing** so POWERFUL,

nothing so STRONG—

GOD'S LOVE is too HIGH

and too DEEP and too LONG!

If I dove
in a **submarine**
under the sea
in a clever disguise,
would GOD'S LOVE **follow** me?

YES!

GOD'S LOVE is EVERYWHERE:
desert, moon, beach . . .
there's **no place** at all
that HIS LOVE cannot reach!

If I did what I shouldn't
(like sometimes I do),
would it mean that it's over,
and GOD'S LOVE is through?

No!

GOD'S LOVE doesn't change
with the **words** that you say

or the **things** that you do.
It will not go away!

You are LOVED and FORGIVEN.
What a wonderful thing!
You're adopted as God's own.
YOU'RE A CHILD OF THE KING!

See, **nothing** can separate you from GOD'S LOVE.
Nothing on earth, or below, or above.

There is **nothing**
so powerful,
nothing so strong—
GOD'S LOVE
is too high and too deep
and too long!